Keeping Fit

WRITTEN BY **Sonja Dunn** ILLUSTRATED BY **John Sandford**

📖 GoodYearBooks

Mike, Mike,
ride that bike.

Rose, Rose,
kiss your toes.

Jack, Jack,
run the track.

Di, Di,
touch the sky.

Peg, Peg,
shake a leg.

Paul, Paul,
kick the ball.

Make a hit
by keeping fit!